The Cloak

Wanda Luthman

Contents

The Cloak

"It's mine. Hand it over," the soldier demanded. Kicking the dirt, the soldier in command handed over the wool cloak. "Ha, ha, it's mine now!" the soldier said as he threw one side over his left shoulder. It opened up, flowed across his back and landed upon him softly, magnificently enveloping him. He tied the leather strings together at his neck, appearing regal now.

The criminal struggled to breathe as he looked down at the man. He mustered all his remaining energy to push himself up on the small piece of wood his feet were nailed to so he could gather his breath. He whispered, "It is yours now. My only earthly possession, I give to you. Bless you, my son."

The soldier, feeling larger than life, paraded around the foot of the cross

showing off to his friends, not hearing a word the criminal had said.

The day drew to a close and the sun sank low in the sky as the criminal took his last breath.

The ground trembled with great force beneath them. Earthquakes were common in the area, so the soldier thought nothing of it. He headed home, satisfied that his work was done. He walked into his grand house, unlatched his dusty sandals and hung the cloak on the hook near the door.

His wife called him to the dinner table and they ate their meal with the usual chatter about the day.

The wife noticed the new garment on the hook and asked, "Did you purchase a new cloak today, dear? It's beautiful but it looks a bit…um,…used." She wrinkled her nose.

"No, I didn't have to purchase it because I won it in a lottery at the crucifixion today," he declared proudly. "Isn't it magnificent? That poor man won't be needing it any longer." He smirked, and his wife nodded in agreement as if this were just another normal daily conversation.

The couple finished their lovely dinner and went to bed. The soldier found sleep quickly, but his dreams were filled with anguish. He awoke in a puddle of sweat, struggling for air. He sat for a moment trying to regain his composure. When he couldn't fall back to sleep, he got up to get a drink of water from the kitchen.

He pumped some fresh water into a ceramic cup and turned to lean against the counter. Wiping the sweat from his brow, he gulped the liquid down in seconds. It was refreshing to his dry throat. A memory from the day flashed through his mind: the man on the cross had asked for water. But, no one obliged. Instead, he'd been offered vinegar. He ran his tongue inside his bottom lip and thought how dry the man's throat must have been. Brushing that thought away, he took another sip from his cup and spat the liquid into the air. It tasted like vinegar. Fear gripped him and he threw the cup to the floor.

Across the room the moonlight shone through the window, illuminating the cloak. He stared at it and wondered about the man it had belonged to. He crossed the floor and ran his fingers over the surface of the cloak. It was made of the finest material, woven wool. He suddenly felt a deep love for the garment and lifted it gently from the hook, noticing the weight of it for the first time. It was just heavy enough to boast the exquisite quality of the material. He held it up for a closer look and then he saw it: dried blood on the inside. He remembered how the man had struggled to carry the cross to the hill. His cloak had been around him and had dragged along the ground, yet it wasn't tattered or dirty. He knew the man had been whipped before being led to his death but hadn't thought about how the man's blood would have been left behind on the cloak. But now, the man was gone, and his blood, that had flowed freely just a few hours before from fresh wounds, had dried and was left on the garment.

It had been a long night standing at the door of Pontius Pilate's Grand Hall and then later controlling the crazy crowds who had screamed, "Crucify Him! Crucify Him!" He assumed the people had good reason for wanting to end this man's life. *He must have been a bad man to be so hated.*

But, now, he wondered if his assumptions were true. The man took his beating with cries of pain but never showed any anger. He carried his cross, falling and struggling, but never showed an ounce of anger. He hung on the cross, dying from pain and exhaustion, but never showed anger.

The soldier ran his hands over the garment again. The beautiful cloak was all his now, but he was compelled to know more about the man who'd once worn it. This so-called 'enemy of the Jews.' He threw it around his shoulders. Again, it fell about him, a perfect fit. He didn't even care that it had another man's blood on it. He loved the beautiful cloak.

The soldier left his home in search of the crucified man's friends. He found none. They had all scattered. He remembered the man's mother crying at the foot of the cross while he so arrogantly marched around wearing his new prized possession. A pain gripped his heart as he thought about the callousness of his actions.

How must this have made the woman feel? Her grown child was dying, and the soldier who was partaking in his death was bragging about winning his cloak right in front of her. Perhaps she had been the one to purchase it, a mother's gift for her son?

The soldier continued to ask around and finally found the address of the woman's home. He arrived at her door and knocked. He reflected on the fact that whomever answers the door might feel in danger and the irony of it struck him. Here he was, a Roman soldier, standing on the doorstep of a condemned criminal's home.

A soft creak sounded and a beautiful, meek woman answered the door. Her face was tired, her eyes red, and dried tears covered her cheeks. Her eyes widened for a moment as if in recognition of the soldier standing before her.

"Ma'am, I'm sorry to bother you at such an hour, but I can't sleep. I won your son's cloak in a drawing, but I'm not sure it truly belongs to me. I need to know more about the man who once wore it. Can you please tell me about your son?"

The woman appeared to breathe a sigh of relief. She lowered her eyes for a moment and humbly curtsied as she invited the soldier inside.

"Yes, please come in, sir."

He walked into her small home and took a seat on a wooden chair in the corner. Compassion filled his heart as he stared into her soulful eyes.

"You see, my boy was quite special, being born under unusual circumstances. I was betrothed when an angel told me I would carry the child of the 'Most High'. I became pregnant before I was wed, but I had not had relations with a man. This was prophesied in our Holy Scrolls." She offered a soft smile and looked off into the distance as if picturing herself in a moment from the past.

"He grew up as any other child and his father and I loved him dearly. He was a good boy—kind and loving. But my son had an incredible gift. He was able to perform miracles. As he aged, he began to study the Holy Scrolls and spent most of his time at the temple. All the scribes and priests knew him and they felt he had a bright future in the employment of the church. At age thirty, he traveled out into the desert on his pilgrimage, a usual process for a holy leader. When he returned, he was even more empowered. He quoted the Holy Scrolls and told parables that explained deep, spiritual truths. We all felt a stirring in our hearts when he spoke. We knew he was special. He performed many miracles of healing. He fed five thousand people in one day with just two fish and three loaves. He raised people from the dead. My son did nothing to deserve death. Unfortunately, the fact that he claimed to be God did not rest well with the scribes and priests. They didn't believe him, but I knew he spoke the truth. He fulfilled all the prophecies for our Messiah. He was the one we had been waiting for. But, now, he's dead," her voice trailed off and her eyes filled with tears.

The soldier released a breath he'd been holding as the woman told her story. A fantastic story about a wonderful man. A man who didn't deserve to die. He looked down at the dirt floor, his shoulders slumped. The cloak felt as though it weighed a thousand pounds on his shoulders.

Tears welled in his eyes. "It's a beautiful cloak, ma'am. I'm sorry for my insolent behavior before. I didn't know your son. I thought He was a common criminal. I don't deserve this. It probably cost you a year's salary. Please," he said as he allowed it to slip from his shoulders, "take it. You should have it." He held it out to her.

She shook her head as she dried her tears with her apron. She pushed his hand with the cloak back toward him.

"No. You mustn't return it to me. My son said it belongs to you now. He told you this as he hung on the cross. He wanted you to have it. He even blessed you. Didn't you hear him?"

The man's voice trembled. "No, ma'am. I'm sorry. I must have been so excited about winning the cloak…," he replied and dropped his head. "I've been a fool. I…I don't deserve it."

The woman reached out and cupped the soldier's shaking hand. "You know, my son used to talk to people who felt they didn't deserve anything either. You know what he told them? He said he loves us so very much that he gave up his kingdom in heaven and came to Earth to prove this love. He came to give us life pressed down, shaken together, and overflowing," she explained.

A tear slid down the soldier's cheek. "Your son sounds like an extraordinary man. How can I be worthy of his cloak?" he asked.

"You simply give thanks and wear it humbly. You accept his forgiveness of your sins and receive his blessings. You wrap the cloak around you and feel his love enveloping you. Then you take that love and share it with others. Bless others who feel they aren't deserving either. And forgive others, just as you have been forgiven. Go…go and live your life free from guilt. Let your heart be full of love for everyone you meet. Let the love of God reside in you and shine for the world to see. My son's cloak will remind you of this. In fact, that's why he died, to show us all how to love unconditionally. Therefore, go in the knowledge of his love," she said standing up.

The soldier stood up too. He threw the cloak over his shoulder, feeling its weight wrapping him in warmth against the spring chill.

"Thank you, ma'am, for sharing this story with me. Your son was an amazing man and you are a generous woman. You have shown me love and compassion that I did not deserve. I want to do just as you say. I want to love others and do good, blessing everyone I meet. Thank you for this gift of love, and for your son's cloak."

"You are most welcome. Everything is as it should be now, the way my son would have wanted it to be. I'm glad to hear you have a new outlook on your life. I believe you shall wear his cloak worthily. You have blessed me by coming here this night and asking about my son," she said.

The soldier drew her into his arms and they embraced for a long moment, holding the mutual love of her son between them. The moment passed, and he looked into her eyes once again. "What was your son's name?" he asked.

"It's Jesus. The son of God," she replied.

"Jesus. I believe he was the son of God. Thank you. I will speak of your son wherever I go. Good-bye, and may you be blessed as you have blessed me this night," the soldier said. He tied the cloak around his neck and walked out the door.

"You as well," she replied.

Just as she went to close the door behind him, she thought she saw the cloak ruffle around the man as if embracing him. It was then she knew in her heart that she had done exactly what her son would have wanted, show the man love and mercy. She no longer felt alone because she knew through the power of love, her son was still alive. Little did she know, her son would be actually alive and well again in three days and the world would never be the same because love had come to earth.

The End

Want to Know More?

If you would like to know the love that the soldier experienced in this story, you can. All you have to do is believe that Jesus is the Son of God and ask him to forgive you of your sins and invite Him into your heart to live.

In Romans Chapter 10, verses 9 and 10 it says, "…that if you confess with your mouth the Lord Jesus and believe in your heart that God has raised Him from the dead, you will be saved. For with the heart one believes unto righteousness, and with the mouth, confession is made unto salvation."

Pray this prayer, "Dear Jesus, I believe you are the Son of God who died and rose again on the third day to forgive us of our sins. I ask you, today, to please forgive me of my sins and come into my heart to live that I might have salvation and eternal life in you. Amen."

Now, you are saved. Go and spread His love in all the world.

~

Author Bio

Wanda Luthman is an international multi-award-winning author. She's been a Christian since she was three years old, was baptized at twelve years old, and attended a Christian College in the Midwest double majoring in Psychology and Sociology.

She has practiced in the field of counseling for over 20 years. But, she felt she really *'met'* God in her late forties when her Pastor taught her contemplative listening which is a Christian form of meditation. Since then, she's been on a mission to share God's love with everyone she meets.

* 9 7 8 1 7 3 4 0 0 9 9 2 7 *